MURDER & MAYHEM CAN BE FUN

Ellen Burrell

To Jim & Barb
Thanks for the memories
But many friendships have
endured so long
Ellen

iUniverse, Inc.
New York Lincoln Shanghai

MURDER & MAYHEM CAN BE FUN

iUniverse books may be ordered through booksellers or by contacting:

iUniverse
2021 Pine Lake Road, Suite 100
Lincoln, NE 68512
www.iuniverse.com
1-800-Authors (1-800-288-4677)

This is a work of fiction. All of the characters, names, incidents, organizations, and dialogue in this novel are either the products of the author's imagination or are used fictitiously.

ISBN: 978-0-595-43705-4 (pbk)
ISBN: 978-0-595-88037-9 (ebk)

Printed in the United States of America

INTRODUCTION

This is a group of games suitable for parties, luncheons and dinner theatre. I have included suggestions for invitations and some suggestions for planning the menu.

To begin, simply copy the pages with numbered clues. You should give each participant 1 clue. If you have fewer guests than clues, give out the clues until they are all gone. Some guests will have more than 1, so make sure that the clues are read in order and no fair peeking at the extra clue until required. Some of the games will require you find someone to play specific parts. Encourage audience participation in all games.

The party host should read each game and the introduction to each game before the game begins in order to be able to answer questions.

Read the direction for each game. For some, the format changes and more information will need to be copied to include with your invitations.

For each game, it is up to the participants to discover: who was the murderer, what was the weapon and what was the motive.

The party host will decide how to determine the winner.

Enjoy and have fun. Murder and Mayhem can be fun.

GAME # 1

THE
BIRTHDAY
PARTY

SUGGESTION FOR INVITATION

Last Night at poor Yorek's birthday party there was an unfortunate incident. The police have asked that we try to recreate the scene.

Everyone who was present at the birthday party has been invited to share their thoughts and observations surrounding the unfortunate demise of poor Yorek.

PLACE:
    TIME:
    DAY:
    PLEASE RSVP
    TELEPHONE:

SUGGESTION FOR INVITATION

Murder most foul has been committed. Last night at Yorek's birthday party someone murdered Yorek and the police believe that those who attended his party may be able to shed some light on the solving of this crime.

Since you were present at the birthday party, they ask that you please attend this lunch to share your observations and perhaps help discover who would do such a crime.

TIME:
    DATE:
    PLACE:
    PLEASE RSVP
    TELEPHONE:

INTRODUCTION: The party host will send out invitations. Remind everyone that because they were at Yorek's birthday party, the police feel they may have seen or be aware of circumstances that may relate to the murder.

Information party host may need for questions from the guests.

Yorek and Mattie have been married for more than 70 years. They have one child, a girl named Tilly. Neither has been married before. In their long devoted marriage, they were fortunate to have Tilly to take care of them.

Tilly never married, never had a boyfriend and had no outside interests. For the last 50 years, she has been everything to Yorek and Mattie. Mattie takes care of all personal problems for Yorek. Yorek sometimes forgets that he is allergic to seafood, perfume and nuts, among other things. Mattie makes sure that he does not come in contact with any.

Tilly is now 70 and has never gone on a vacation or left home for any more than a few hours unless she is taking care of her parents. Because of Yorek's allergies, there have never been pets allowed in the house.

The party host will read the introduction and then go by the numbers for each to read his or her clue.

MURDER MYSTERY DINNER

The Party Host: Alas! Dear Yorek, I knew him well. Struck down in his prime of life at his own birthday party, his 95th. Detectives have not determined the cause of death, but feel there is something not quite right. You have been invited tonight because you were all present at this noble man's party. His grieving widow is out now with their only child, Tilly, choosing the casket.

Did poor Yorek die of natural causes, was he murdered, was it somehow an accident or was it suicide? Did any one see anything strange at the party?

Each of you has been given an envelope with a number. Inside you will find a suggestion or comment for you to share with everyone. You may add your own comments and others may question you. I will answer any questions I can.

You must determine who did it. How it was done and why. Have fun and remember there is a prize. At the end, please fill out the ballot. The correct answers will be placed in a bowl and the winner will be drawn from these.

1. Now I was at the party and we were all having a great time. The fruit punch had more sparkle as the evening wore on. To be honest with you though, I thought it was the heat from the candles that did him in.

2. That was quite a blaze wasn't it. Once Yorek figured out what the blaze was all about, he blew them out. It took some time, but he got the job done. Must have been the punch give him those energies.

3. Maybe Mattie added a little Geritol to the coffee. He might have done cartwheels if she put enough in.

4. It wasn't the Geritol done the job it was the alcohol. I didn't see who did it, but by gosh it sure did liven up the party. All that dancing was enough to give everyone a heart attack. What do you call that murder, suicide or an accident?

5. None of the above! I still think Yorek ate something he shouldna. Maybe he was allergic to those shrimps or peanuts. Everybody seems to be allergic to nuts these days.

6. Yeah, but something like that wouldn't put that smile on his face. No it's gotta be the punch. Who spiked the punch?

7. I did! But I've done it before and all it did was make everyone happy.

8. It has got to do with him getting all hot and bothered, blowing out the candles. That's a big job for an old man. The smile was because he made it this far and that old song did make him feel like a jolly good fellow.

9. He was probably happy because he was able to eat something he liked without being told it wasn't good for him. Mattie was having such a good time, she didn't watch his every bite. I think he secretly wanted to eat all the shellfish and nuts on the table for just one last time.

10. But that would be suicide. He wasn't ready to die yet. It has got to be something else. Maybe his heart just couldn't take all the excitement.

11. Mattie moved most of the dishes that had shellfish and nuts in them out of his reach so he wouldn't see them.

12. There are other things that he may have been allergic to, like the flowers on the table. He did stay away from those.

13. If it wasn't all those things on the table or in the food, what's left. It means that we can rule out an accident or suicide and that leaves murder. But who? What else was he allergic to that was here?

14. If it was murder, then it had to be someone who would have a reason to want him gone. Who would have a motive? And who would have the means? It would have to be something at the party perhaps there was a dish with peanut oil in it.

Party Host: A police report has just come in. According to the coroner, Yorek had a heart attack while in anaphylactic shock. In other words, he was allergic to something he ingested by breathing or eating it. They have examined his stomach contents and have found nothing that would cause an allergic reaction. They have not found any pollen in his breathing passages and believe the source to be air borne.

15. Perfume or cologne, was anyone wearing it? Did he get too close to someone wearing it?

16. I was wearing perfume and we did dance together. But he didn't even sniffle while we were dancing.

17. I heard him sneeze a few times, but that was later in the evening. It was after he blew out the candles on the cake. Maybe the cake had something in it. Maybe there was something from the candles.

18. Who brought the cake? Where was it bought? I thought it was delicious and I didn't notice anything strange about it.

Party Host: Another police report. We checked with the bakery. The ingredients were safe. No nuts and no peanut oil. The candles were put on after it was picked up.

19. That leaves the candles. Who put the candles on the cake? What kind of candles were they?

20. Mattie and I went together to buy the candles and we bought the only ones we could find that had that many all the same. You don't know how hard it is to find 95 candles that are the same. We didn't check to see if they had anything on them, but I didn't notice anything at the time.

21. When Tilly brought the cake in, she arranged the candles. I watched her and I helped her light them later. I have never seen candles so pretty and with such a lovely scent.

22. Tilly has always been so close to Mattie and Yorek, helpful you know. She's an only child, never married. She's the only one left, she and Mattie.

Party Host: Fill out your ballots now. Who, How and Why. Then sign your name and put it in the bowl. Remember your answer must include all details.

GAME #2

THE
STORY
BOOK
CAPER

Game #2 THE STORY BOOK CAPER

This was a luncheon for a group of ladies. When we contacted the restaurant, we explained what we were going to do and they offered to add to the enjoyment by providing a mystery lunch. The ladies not only had to wait for the fun to begin, but each part of the lunch was a surprise as well. By the end of the third course, they were guessing what the next would be.

Since this was the monthly meeting of the group, no invitations were necessary. The notice was included in their monthly newsletter. To set up this game, you will need a tree, a small Christmas tree will do, several small hats as decoration on the tree and the clues glued or taped onto to each hat (one per hat). The hats should be numbered and the clue presented as the number is called. There should be 2 prizes at least. One prize will go to the person who chooses the hat that instructs him/her to die. One prize will go to the first person who can state the murderer, the motive (exactly) and the weapon. More prizes may be given out at the host's discretion.

Please note: directions are given in bold or italic letters are not to be read.

MURDER MYSTERY LUNCHEON

The party host: The object of the game is to discover through observation, intuition and clues—Who did it; The motive; and The weapon. Just to keep you alert, you are going to provide the special effects. Whenever we talk about the wind blowing, Group number one will wail with the wind. Group number two screams when appropriate. Whenever we have groups talking about the situation, Group number three buzzes as do the bees gathered around a clover patch. Group number four ooo's and ah's when appropriate. Each group must listen for their prompt, then with feeling provide the sound effects. And so, our story begins:

The night was dark and dreary. The wind blew sounding like the sirens of the night with their wailing. The lady's group huddled together to walk home, there is safety in numbers. They feared the darkness of the night with its strange noises. A huge gust of wind blew their hats away into a large tree. They watched helplessly and huddled closer. They decided to join in groups to discuss the situation. Part of group 3 goes up to the tree to assess the problem.

A representative from group 3 goes to the party host and says: "Oh what will we do, what will we do?"

The party host steps up to the tree and says: Now see here Mr. Tree, I really do appreciate that you have been able to catch our hats in your lovely branches, but would you please, please release them now. **Group 4 ooo's and ah's.**

The party host steps forward and gently pulls one hat out of the branches.

The party host: Well that wasn't so bad was it. Now may we all carefully take one hat each from your branches. The tree has agreed to allow everyone to take a hat, but you must keep the clue or suggestion secret until you are asked to share it with the group. At this time, I must tell you that one of you is in danger. Be careful. Should an accident happen, it is up to everyone of you to try to solve the crime. The clues must be carefully considered and when you think you can solve the mystery BUZZZ or WHISTLE. You may have one guess only. If you are wrong, you are eliminated and the game continues.

The hats are numbered and we will listen to the clues in numeric order. There is a prize for the one who solves the crime first. If no one has solved the crime after all clues are read, I will answer any questions for you until someone has the answer. Remember, not all of the clues are relevant to the solving of the mystery, some are red herrings. But you should be able tell what hints are helpful and which are not.

Have fun. If after the crime has been solved, you would like some of the clues explained, I will be happy to do so. The victim will read his/her note as soon as she has recovered.

1. A lot of movies have their beginnings in the fairy tales and nursery rhymes of our childhood. This game is very similar and some clues are based on them.

2. Mother Goose loves to see her children at play. She should be given credit for many of the overbearing attitudes of men. Such as Peter who kept his wife in a pumpkin shell.

3. Wicked step mothers are in fairy tales and are depicted as cruel tyrants and murderers. As in Snow White, Cinderella, Sleeping Beauty and Rapunzel.

4. **DO NOT READ Say nothing, scream and die. You will get your reward in heaven. You will be able to read this note after the game is over.**

Party Host: Oh my goodness. We have a problem here. A murder to solve. The first to do so from the clues wins.

5. Animals are also on the storybook hit lists. Mother Hubbard starved her dog, everyone was out to get the big, bad wolf, the beast had to prove himself a handsome loving prince before a witch's spell could be broken, and don't forget Foxy Loxy.

6. The big bad wolf was busy blowing down houses—he didn't do it.

7. Snow White's wicked step mother tried to do her in with a poisoned apple, would she do the same to one of us.

8. The wicked witch from sleeping beauty used a similar weapon as was used today.

9. BoPeep was upset because she missed the junior prom, her date was fast asleep in the haystack.

10. The hunters in primitive cultures dipped their spears in this.

11. Red Riding Hood missed the junior prom because she had to take some flowers to her grandmother.

12. Was Little Boy Blue only asleep in the hay?

13. CSI has said that the preferred murder weapon of women is poison.

14. Did Little Boy Blue prick his finger on the needle in the haystack?

15. Jack and Jill never made it to the prom. Jack thinks someone pushed him.

16. Red's grandmother was a member of the lady's group.

17. Hide and seek I am hidden in the haystack and I am similar to the murder weapon.

18. The ladies attending the races in 'My Fair Lady' certainly needed one to hold their hats in place.

19. A small piece of red material was found at the murder scene.

20. The thunder roared, the lightning flashed and all the world was shaken, the little pig picked up his tail and ran home to save his bacon. The three pigs were busy stopping another big wind.

21. A bottle with a small amount of mysterious liquid was found outside the murder scene.

22. Red loved her grandmother very much, if only she didn't want so much.

23. Note from the Old Woman Who Lived in a Shoe. I would have murdered the little brat first if I had known. She complained about my poor living quarters.

24. Some of the ladies in the parade in 'Hello Dolly' needed one to keep their hats in place.

25. Finger prints from a dainty hand were found on the bottle.

26. I didn't like the little brat either, she told people I starved my dog note from Old Mother Hubbard.

27. Little Red Riding Hood's grandmother had a very busy day. First the Woodsman came and took care of the big bad wolf and then Red brought her flowers, such a thoughtful child, and then she had a meeting with her lady's group.

28. They are all grandmothers, said the murderer, I don't care which one I get.

29. Bo Peep came gunning for the murderer when she found out about the needle in the haystack. The murderer said she was only practicing, she didn't put enough poison on the needle to harm Little Boy Blue.

30. The poor dear child, missing her prom and all, her grandmother should have waited another day for her flowers and she didn't need Red's date, the woodsman. Grandma should have stuck to beating up big bad wolves.

Who did it? What was the weapon? What was the motive?

GAME #3

THE
PERILS
OF
FAITH

SUGGESTION FOR INVITATION

You are invited to be in the audience of the Chantelle Robert Talk Show. For this evening she will be interviewing a notorious wife abuser—Calvin Walker—and his estranged wife—Faith Simmons. Calvin has made some rather outrageous statements that the police are trying to confirm. He, of course, is trying to save his own neck. Come and be a part of the audience. You will have an opportunity to ask questions and voice your opinion.

We do not want Calvin thinking that women should be pushovers for a fast line.

Calvin may biting off more than he can chew by asking for this chance to state his side of the story.

The fun begins at
    TIME:
    DATE:
    PLACE:
    RSVP

    TELEPHONE:

GAME #3 PERILS OF FAITH

NOTES: To the party host The story that leads to the talk show may be sent as part of the invitation or read at the party.

For this game, you will have to assign parts by name instead of by numbers.

Faith Walker—wife of Calvin—owner and president of Simmons Shoes Inc.
Calvin Walker—unfaithful husband of Faith—lover of Penny
Penny Thomas—Calvin's paramour and co-conspirator
David/Diane Larson—company lawyer
Jonathon/Joanna Clark—company accountant
Jasper Collins—company bookkeeper
Chantelle Robert—talk show host
Detective—who comes in after the murder
Rescuer who has been invited by Chantelle to fill in details when necessary
The rest of the guests will act as the studio audience. They should be encouraged to question any of the participants in regards to the murder.

The story that leads to the talk show.

Faith and her father ran a successful business as partners. Calvin jointed the firm and fell madly in love with the boss's daughter. He courted her, took her to all the fancy places he could think of. He did not enjoy plays, music concerts or the ballet, but she did. He planned his attack well and although he was bored, he continued on to the master plan.

When he felt that he had her confidence, he asked her to marry him. He was only a little disturbed by Faith insisting on a pre-nuptial agreement.

Okay, fine so he wouldn't get anything if they ever divorced. He would remain the true and loving husband until he managed to milk the company for everything he could. All he had to do was get rid of the company watchdogs, the accountant, Jonathon Clark; the lawyer, David Larson and, of course, Daddy.

Daddy passed away unexpectedly leaving the company to Faith and leaving Calvin an open door. He really did not do anything to hurry Daddy's death.

Unfortunately, Daddy died of natural causes.

Calvin now had his chance to hoodwink a few people. His first target was the bank manager. He went in with forged papers to declare himself a signing authority for the company.

He couldn't wait to inform Penny Thomas of his new domain. Penny Thomas was trusted neighbor and friend to Faith. She was obviously more than a friend to Calvin.

Calvin started spending like there was no tomorrow. New clothes, a new car and one for Penny and this was just the beginning.

But then, in stepped Jasper Collins, bookkeeper. You see Jasper had worked for the company for several years and was on top of everything. He knew when the secretary spent too much on paper clips, never mind new clothes and cars on Calvin's new expense account. Jasper brought the unusual expenses to the attention of the accountant, who in turn informed the lawyer. The trio went immediately to the bank manager to discuss the situation.

Why was he suddenly accepting cheques signed by Calvin? Well, he or his staff had not done anything wrong, he had the papers to prove that everything was above board. A quick examination of the papers, and Calvin was in hot water. Because the papers did not include the David Larson's signature, they were not legal.

The bank manager started to turn a strange shade of purple and produced a collection of cheques that were about to be honored. Calvin was a busy boy. David insisted that the cheques be returned to the payees and that all cheques signed by Calvin be copied for evidence and returned.

Real Estate on the lake, close to Faith's cottage, a hide away in bush country and his own condo in town. All his plans were destroyed. Finding out that his plans were somewhat curtailed disturbed Calvin. Unrepentantly, he no longer had his expense account and if he wasn't careful, he would no longer have his meal ticket.

He went straight to Penny. He had to do something before the accountant and the lawyer got to Faith. Faith was on her way home from the city, he would call her and waylay her to the cottage where he could carry out his immediate plans before being found out.

He took Faith for a midnight canoe ride. Complete with lunch, wine and a sweet desert, made especially for the occasion by Penny. The plan was that they would have a wonderful moonlight paddle out on the lake. After a midnight lunch, they would go in for a swim. Faith would be dizzy from the desert and would become disoriented. Calvin would paddle back to the cottage and when he was sure that Faith would have drowned, he called 911.

If he called too soon, there was a chance they would find her alive and actually rescue her.

The rescue units arrived at the cottage early in the morning and took down the details of the accident. A broken hearted Calvin and a very sad Penny wasted no time in tearfully relating the details. They hadn't counted on one little fact. Faith had been an olympic hopeful and had practiced in that lake. She could find her way back to the beach blindfolded. And as she walked out of the water, Penny screamed and Calvin watched in shock.

The rescuers made sure that she was safe and then left.

But now Calvin was getting desperate. He did not have much time. He had to do something fast.

Poor Calvin, he never did understand women.

Faith was suspicious of him when David called her about the bank problem. She was no body's fool, she let David know every move. That night, Calvin, believe it or not tried again. He made a path along the cliff very wet and muddy and then proposed they have dinner at a local restaurant. They could walk home along the path and Faith would slip and fall on the mud and down the cliff. Too bad, so sad.

Everything was going well. Calvin managed to put sleeping powders in Faith's wine while she was admiring the scenery. When dinner arrived, she sat down and they made a toast to each other. Faith just sipped at her wine. Calvin took his down in one swallow.

Suddenly Calvin gasped, he was choking on a piece of meat. Faith reacted immediately. She positioned herself behind him and performed the Heimlich Maneuver. To sooth his throat, she reached out for a glass of wine, hers. They left the restaurant immediately for their walk down the path.

Faith rushed down to call 911.

Calvin had slipped on some mud and was hanging onto a tree just over the cliff. Penny was shocked that it was Faith calling for help. Calvin was rescued unharmed except for a few bruises.

The next morning, he was ready to try again. This time with the help of Faith's dog, Rufus and Penny's nephew with cat in hand. The plan was that on her regular walk in the bush with Rufus, a Newfoundland retriever, the nephew would throw the cat on the walk in front of him and the resulting crashing run through the bush would cause fatal injuries to Faith.

Faith was preparing for the walk. Calvin had decided to go with her to make sure all went according to plan. Just as they were leaving, Faith had to tie her shoe. She gave the leash to Calvin to hold.

The cat hissed at Rufus, Rufus took off after it. Calvin was dragged, well let's just say he went faster than he has ever gone before and he saw more trees and rocks than ever before.

When rescuers found him, the cat was up a tree with Rufus proudly barking down below. Calvin was still with him in body if not in spirit. He was tangled up in branches and the dog leash and he was badly injured. A few broken bones, scopes, bruises and cuts and very disoriented. Then, to add insult to injury, he and Penny were arrested for attempted murder.

The police found evidence of all Calvin's accidents. It doesn't matter that his plans backfired on him. The intent was there.

Penny was willing to be his well taken care of paramour, but not his accomplice in murder. She told all and slam dunked poor Calvin.

Calvin arranged this talk show in order to try to appeal to the public. How could he be charged with attempted murder? He was the injured party. Faith wasted no time freeing herself from Calvin and testified at his trial. The final blow came when Penny and her nephew also testified.

CHANTELLE ROBERT TALK SHOW

Party Host comes in and asks the guests to join in a lunch: The show is setting up, you are invited to join the staff for a lunch.

Party Host should make sure this is followed. Stage Direction: While everyone is milling around, Jasper is greeting the crowd. He has come with a large supply of candies to share. It is the one joy he has, he loves to come to company parties. He is a lonely gentle old man who is getting ready for retirement. At every company party, he is a welcome sight because he draws people together with his conversation and the candies he is never without. He puts candies in several of the dishes on the tables and also on the stage tables.

The stage is set up with a table and two chairs. When Calvin comes in he starts to eat the candies on the table. They are his favorites.

Party host: Tonight Chantelle is interviewing notorious wife abuser, Calvin Walker and his estranged wife Faith Simmons. During the evening, you will meet a police detective, a rescuer who went to Calvin's aid, Jasper the bookkeeper at Faith's office, Calvin's paramour, Penny, the lawyer and the accountant at Faith's office. Be observant, watch everyone and everything. You are now witnesses to murder and mayhem.

As the lights flicker, everyone finds a seat.

Chantelle: Good evening! My guests tonight are Calvin Walker and Faith Simmons. In our studio audience is Penny Thomas, the other woman, Jasper the bookkeeper, David Larson the lawyer, Jonathon Clark the accountant and various members of our police force and the rescue team. Calvin let me start with you. Why did you do all these rather despicable things.

Calvin: I didn't do anything, it was all Faith's doing.

Chantelle: OOOO—And does that include Penny Thomas, did she help you or Faith. I understand she avoided prison by telling all.

Calvin: Harlot! I loved my wife. Penny blinded me. She seduced me. They made a deal with the devil.

Penny: Liar, pig, You came to me!

Chantelle: Please Penny, everyone will have their chance to speak. Let's start with the first accident. Would you tell us what happened, Calvin.

Calvin: Well we had a pleasant little paddle out on the lake. Faith stood up after lunch and some wine and fell overboard. I heard a thump and a splash. I tried to find her, I called out to her and I paddled around looking for her. When I couldn't find her I paddled straight for home to call for help.

Chantelle: And you Faith?

Faith: We were supposed to go on a romantic midnight swim together after lunch. I dove in after having lunch and the wine and Calvin was to follow and swim with me. I thought that the cake tasted funny so I just put it in the water. It was one of Penny's special cakes. It had a lot of rich frosting flowers on it. Calvin seemed anxious for me to eat it. And I'll bet he didn't waste any time paddling back to her after I disappeared.

Chantelle: You think the cake was doped?

Faith: Sure do! Penny admitted it in court.

Calvin: It was one of Penny's specialties. You see she wanted to get rid of my dear wife.

Penny: You asked me to do it. You didn't want her to survive the midnight swim.

Chantelle: Faith, how did you survive?

Faith: I swam back. I was an Olympic hopeful and that lake was where I practiced. I could find my way back to the cottage blindfolded.

Chantelle: Let's move on shall we? The next incident was at Marino's Restaurant was it not? I understand you drugged Faith's wine and you poured water on the path to make it slippery.

Calvin: Yeah, well you see, the doctor said she needed to relax after Daddy passed away. I only wanted to help her.

Chantelle: And the mud?

Calvin: I just wanted to wash some garbage off the path.

Chantelle: Wasn't that part of a larger plan?

Faith: Why certainly it was. Why don't you tell her why this plan backfired on you?

Chantelle: Go on Faith, what happened?

Faith: He started to choke on some food and I helped him spit it up. Afterwards, I gave him a glass of wine to drink. Mine. Then while we were walking home along the cliffs, Calvin became dizzy and slipped. He was able to grab a tree on the way down, it saved his life. But it was an accident meant for me.

Chantelle: Now Calvin, it seems you fell into another one of your traps.

Calvin: Yeah, well. she knew the wine was drugged. She did it on purpose.

Faith: Don't you worry darling since getting rid of you, my nerves have calmed right down. The doctor says it has done wonders for me.

Chantelle: Oh, but that's not the end of the story. Wasn't there another accident?

Faith: Yes, just a little incident with my dog, Rufus.

Penny: That dam dog dragged Calvin half way across the county!

Faith: Defending your lover now, Penny? A short while ago he was a liar and a pig.

Chantelle: Good point, Faith, But let's hear more about this accident. What did happen?

Faith: We were just going out for a little walk with Rufus. My shoe was untied so I gave Calvin the leash. He put the loop over his hand. Then I heard a cat. While you see, Rufus is normally kind and gentle, but he hates cats.

Chantelle: Ouch! What kind of dog?

Penny: It was a monster. On purpose she got this monster.

Faith: Newfoundland retriever.

David Larson: The dog was legally licensed and was not on the list of dangerous or vicious dogs. He just happened to hate cats. The cat that provoked Rufus and had him drag Calvin into the bush belonged to Penny.

Faith: Poetic justice, don't you think? Calvin was slam dunked by yet another trap meant for me.

Calvin stands up about to say something and suddenly gasps, holds his stomach, sits down again with a crash. The detective comes forward.

Detective: Mr. Walker is dead. You are all witnesses, please remain in your seats and share your observations with us. You have each been given a piece of paper. All ballots that have the correct solution will be put into a hat and be drawn for prizes. You must have WHO, HOW AND WHY. There will be a short question period after which you must write down your answer.

GAME #4

BARNWICK
HUMBUG
ALL ROUND
COMMITTEE MEMBER
FAMILY GOOF OFF

THE INVITATION

To the people of Pickwick County As you may be aware, Barnwick Humbug has introduced a city by-law restricting the use of rocking chairs. This law was passed at council at the January meeting. Because of the storm that day, not very many council members attended. Those who were present, asked that the passing of this law be delayed until there could be more discussion on it. Barnwick insisted on passing the by-law in order to put cat owners at ease. Furthermore, any cat that comes in contact with a rocking chair should receive compensation through its owner for damages.

The city should consider a slight raise in taxes to help defray the expenses of surgery for the injured cats.

Cats are not the issue, Barnwick, however, is. This is the first time he has pushed his own interests into the public and it should be the last. You are invited to attend and comment on this by-law

TIME:
DATE:
PLACE:

Sherwood Wells will at that time interview Barnwick and give the audience ample opportunity to voice their objections to the new by-law. On his talk show, Sherwood will question Barnwick about his proposal. This will be a live broadcast with national coverage.

GAME #4 BARNWICK HUMBUG

The scene is a stage with a lounge style set up. Two comfortable chairs with a small table and an area rug. This is the set for a talk show. For the party you will need 2 people who will act as Sherwood and Barnwick. The rest of the parts will be given to party guests and read in numeric order. The party host will, when needed, describe the scene and produce any information that comes from other sources. All items in bold are not to be read aloud. They are for instructions only.

Please read over your part in case there are stage directions as per No. 2—This person must poke Barnwick to make sure he is dead. At the end of the game, write down the name of the murderer, the weapon and the motive. All correct answers will be put in a bowl and the winner will drawn from there.

The party host: At the end of the party, put your solutions on a piece of paper. The Murderer, the weapon and the motive, then sign your name. All of the correct solutions will be put in a bowl and the winner will be drawn from there.

The party host: You are the audience and you are here to voice your opinion of Barnwick's barn storming tactics in having pushed a law through committee without proper notification. Sherwood Wells is interviewing the local government official, Barnwick Humbug. Barnwick has been instrumental in having a law created to ban rocking chairs from all public places, which includes front porches if they are accessible by the public. His reasoning for the need of such a law is that all cats are in danger of having their tails mangled by said rockers and we must protect them at all costs.

Sherwood: I understand your cat had a slight accident involving a rocking chair.

Barnwick: Slight accident! Poor Jasper almost had to have surgery to straighten his tail. Rocking chairs are a menace to society. It's a pity that a cat cannot wander at will without having his tail squashed by some mad rocking chair fanatic.

Sherwood: That's a bit harsh don't you think. After all we are only talking about some cat that wouldn't stay home. Perhaps you should have put him on a leash instead.

Barnwick: Cats don't belong on leashes. Leashes are for dogs. Cats should be able to roam where they please. And people with rocking chairs make it dangerous for the poor animals.

Sherwood: Do you mind if we allow your supporters and opponents to comment on your new law? After all you did take advantage of a stormy night when few of the committee members were able to attend.

The Party Host: Barnwick stands up to address the audience and in his own objectionable manner begins a speech designed to say nothing and promise everything. While he is talking, he slips on something on the stage. He falls down as a loud bang is heard.

Barnwick: Good people of Pickwick County, you know I have always had your best interests at heart—Oops.

The Party Host: Barnwick is lying still and shows signs of being more than just injured. The group of people in the audience gathers around.

1. Yep he is a dead duck. Does anybody have a cell phone? We should call the police and an ambulance. I mean call the police, not our bumbling sheriff. He could shoot himself in the foot with all the excitement.

2. Hold on a minute. Are you sure he is dead? Knowing good old Barnwick, he is only playing dead to get our sympathy. Poke him a couple of times to make sure. No, a good poke like this. Hmmm, I guess he bought the big one this time.

Note: Make sure this person pokes Barnwick.

3. But you know, we could probably solve this thing, if we put our heads together. That way when that idiot sheriff arrives, we can hand him all the evidence he needs without him asking too many stupid questions. Hell, we could convince him that one of Barwick's beloved cats got to him.

4. Okay, what do we know? What made him slip? Did he land on anything? Did anybody see someone on the stage before this started? This could be just a slip and fall accident.

5. Would you believe that it looks like cat dirt? He skidded real well in that stuff. When he went down, I heard a loud bang, it came from the curtains back stage. That leaves all of us out. We were out front watching the show.

6. Look here! There's a little round hole in his back. I think he has been shot. He was just getting up to make another one of his boring speeches. It would have to be someone on stage or back of the curtains to shoot him in the back. Nice touch making sure he would slip at the same time.

7. Hey, I put the dirt on the stage. I just wanted him to be reminded of the number of times his cat has done his business in my garden. That cat has ruined more prize roses than bugs. and I couldn't spray the cat. If Barnwick had known that I wanted to spray the cat, he would've added that to the new law.

8. So, who would want him dead? This law isn't the only stupid thing he has done. This past year, he has ignored the voters and all his promises have blown in the wind. I don't know about the rest of you, but I figured some how, some way the majority voters would vote him out of office. It's his family that have kept him in office, more than 50% of voters are related to him. Put a hole in him and no one has to vote for him.

9. What are some of the other stupid things he has done? He has been in office so long and caused so many problems, there must be something that would make someone want to kill him. Just watch him with that cat. I think the cat has been giving him all the answers. If you listen, they purr to each other. The guy was nuts. We need him out of office.

10. What about the time he made Jake cover his calendar at the garage? Mike, the sheriff, went over to the garage with a towel and Jake growled at him. One look at Jake's face was enough to set the sheriff running. Say did the sheriff ever recover from his cold dip the day Barnwick made him retrieve Jasper's binky toy from the river?

11. Never mind the sheriff, what about this poor sap, Sherwood, and the whole TV staff. They had set up this show because Barnwick wanted to get the people's support before the rest of the council made him sit in the corner again.

12. Word has it that he was trying to have even pictures of rocking chairs banned too. He was nutty enough to enforce the law even if his stooge the sheriff refused to obey it.

13. This guy was crazy. He had too many relatives in town for us to vote him out of council and they didn't want to have to support him if he did get the axe by the voters. He was a lazy hoot and would never work for a living. Could be the idea of supporting him was too much to take.

14. Would his relatives want to pay for a funeral instead? Funerals are expensive these days. They would probably throw him in the river downstream and watch him drift out to sea.

15. Harlow, Barnwick's cousin, works here. His only motive would be that he would want Barnwick's cushy job and not even his relatives would go for that. His only good point is that he would sit like a bump on a log and never say a thing, not even if he was asked.

16. The relatives needed him to give their businesses a boost. As long as he passed laws to keep the snoops busy and the sheriff happy, he could stay in office. But the sheriff isn't happy anymore and no one has benefited from all those election promises.

17. We need to find someone who would benefit from Barnwick's death. so far we have grandmothers, (with rocking chairs) gardeners, the sheriff, Jake, Harlow, Barnwick's family and Sherwood there. What about it, Sherwood, did you want him dead?

18. Poor Sherwood is in shock. No one ever ended one of his shows like this. He has had plenty of bummers on his show and usually friends of Barnwick. But his show did go on.

19. The sheriff might be able to shed some light on the situation. If he lost one of his guns or loaned one to someone, he would at least be able to provide another suspect. Where was the sheriff, he didn't stay around to watch the show.

20. He said he had some police business to take care of. He said he had to pick up some groceries for his mother, she was out of cat food. He could have slipped back in to take care of something here while everyone was busy.

21. The sheriff had opportunity and a gun. And he was Barnwick's stooge. If he solved this crime, the town council would let him keep his job. Barnwick was the one who made him look foolish sending him off to settle arguments that should be taken care of over the backyard fence.

22. Barnwick was gearing up for another election. soon he would start making empty promises all over town. His precious cat would be at his side. His family were making plans to deal with Barnwick. The sheriff wanted to deal with the cat, he said the cat should go for a swim underwater. If the family did decide to end Barnwick's political career, they would have to do it soon. Harlow was anxious to find out what their plans are and he would like to prepare to run for council.

23. The sheriff had motive, a gun and opportunity. Jake was certainly mad enough, but that was all. He would paint Barnwick purple before he would shoot him. His family had a lot of reasons to rub him out and just as many reasons to keep him.. The staff and crew considered him a joke, he provided the comedy relief. Sherwood wanted to move on to bigger and better things and being Barnwick's stooge didn't do it for him. Harlow was stupid enough to think he could get away with it and take his place on the town council. Someone on the town council may have been fed up.

24. How about it folks? Who did it, why did he or she do it and what was the weapon?

GAME #5

PLAIN
JANE
BEWARE
ALL
COMPUTERS

INVITATION

Welcome to Star Mobile Systems.

Tonight's meeting will be a discussion on the unfortunate demise of Plain Jane. You have your instructions. Please come prepared. This should be a night to remember.

The inquisition will start at:

TIME:
DATE:
PLACE:

A late buffet lunch. Please bring your favorite dish. Desert and refreshments will be provided by host.

RSVP
TELEPHONE:

Before the party, please study your persona. when you are asked questions about your activities, try to answer them in keeping with your character. during the evening, you will be questioned about your whereabouts and actions, try to make them plausible according to what your character would do. Remember for the evening you are this person.

INSTRUCTIONS FOR PARTY HOST There are speeches and character profiles for up to 12 people. Make sure each guest wears his/her name tag. Put a time limit on the free for all discussion after all parts have been read. You may have to prompt for more discussion. At the end of your allotted time, have each one identify on a piece of paper: Who or what is Plain Jane, who disassembled her, what was the probable weapon and why was it done. Encourage each person to discuss their findings. The winner is the person who has discovered all the answers. Prepare envelopes with each one containing: 1 name tag, 1 character profile, and 1 speech. The party host will start the game by introducing the rules and explaining the game. Have fun.

Party Host: During the game, you can ask questions of anyone in the room. Questions may be directed to anyone. It is up to the people involved to decide how much information they will give when asked. Several of the employees of star Mobile belong to a secret society whose sole purpose is to eliminate inconsistencies within the company. Every aspect of the society is carried out in secret, orders are given, votes are taken and assignments handed out without the knowledge of who other members are. The speech you have been given must be shared at the appropriate time with the rest of the players. The first player who identifies all of the conspirators, the motive, the weapon, who or what was Plain Jane, will win.

NAME TAGS

SEDGEWICK HOLLIS

SMITHERS ARCHY

ZIMPLER ELSPETH

MANLEY LUCINDA

NELSON MILTON

LESTER MILLICENT

CHARACTER PROFILES

You are Sedgewick, a computer engineer with the company. You are very secretive and answer questions directly without giving any extra information. You tell no lies, but you do elaborate on the truth. You prefer yes and no answers. You are very intelligent and are totally independent with one exception. You are a member of the society. You believe in its principles because you work hard to correct any errors in the performance of robots and computers you helped to design. You are very open to people who want to discuss the inner workings of computers on a need to know basis. As you said in your speech, you did not come in to the office early in the evening, but you returned later and performed your part of the crime. You are one of the group who disassembled Jane. It is up to you to avoid detection while seeming to help find the others. It was an order from the society. Your family is very supportive of your work, but there is a strain on your relationship with your wife. She would like to see you home more often. There are too many late nights and not enough time on the weekends to make up for it.

You are Hollis, an accountant with Star Mobile. You only understand computers from the programs you use. You have never been involved with the inner workings of Jane or the computer system. You only use the programs you need to complete your work. You are quiet and like to get straight to work when you come in. Your accounts are always up to date and you are in control of facts and figures. Jane was to you an access tool and a very expensive one. You are not a member of the society and are barely aware of its existence. You have noticed problems with the computers and report them to the appropriate people. When you leave the office, you stop at the coffee spot for your usual flavored coffee and a muffin. You then proceed home to enjoy a quiet evening with your family. Your wife is a stay at home mom and involves you in the care of the children, one boy and one girl. schooling and recreation are the responsibilities of both parents and you consult with each other before decisions are made. You live within your means and are quite comfortable.

You are Smithers, a computer programmer. You have been approached by the Society to be a member. You do not know who put your name up for consideration, but you declined. You go with the flow as a general rule. The computers you program are used mainly in the accounting department. Jane was on a different circuit. Your only involvement with Jane was from your communications outside the company. You do not get involved with the personal lives of your co-workers. Your life is your family. Your job is a means by which you can enjoy family outings every weekend.

You are Archy. You work at Star Mobile as a night watchman. You have no involvement with computers and do not understand their workings. Jane was to you like a companion on the long usually lonely nights. Hearing her buzzings and calls were a comfort. All was well and all systems were running. The employees at Star are friendly and you have no reason to suspect any of them. You know nothing of the secret society. You are single and you have many single friends. some of the women in your life are becoming very chummy and you are starting to think of closer relationships.

You are Zimpler. You are employed as a computer programmer and also sub for the computer engineer in your department. You are a member of the secret society. You insist that things are done right, if not the first time, then keep at it until the system is perfect. Jane was an annoyance to you. She had many glitches that frustrated people. You have on many occasions gone around Jane's loops several times before actually making contact with your intended caller. You are one of the people involved with the demise of Plain Jane. You must keep this a secret while trying to find the others. It is up to you to avoid detection. Your wife is sometimes disturbed by your insistence to have the perfect house and perfect children. You do not understand how someone can survive in a sloppy environment. You demand precision at work and would like more precision at home.

You are Elspeth. You do not understand a lot of what goes on around you. You have not been with the company very long, but from your resume the society decided you could be a very useful member. What no one knows about you is that your resume was embellished with a few unearned records. It won't be long before you are found out and Jane's passing just may be the beginning of the end. You must be careful or you could become a scapegoat. You joined the society not knowing why. Your only interest was being a part of any group and the society's rules intrigued you. Without really understanding what you were doing, you contributed to the dismemberment of Jane. You must now avoid detection not only from your part in the crime but also your false credentials. You tend to be flighty and when your friends questioned you about this job, you shrugged your shoulders and said 'a job is a job'. You don't really care about anything, not your job, not your personal relationships or about controlling your spending binges. You owe the max on most of your credit cards and it doesn't disturb you that you have not been able to pay your monthly commitments. If this job fails, you will simply move on to another.

You are Manley. You are all business. You design protection equipment and the systems which detect intruders. You are not a member of the society and are very distrustful of those people who have chosen to join. You do not know which people in the company have joined the society, but you are always watchful and suspicious. You make sure your crew are alert at all times and you do not permit them to bring strangers into the office. All visitors must wait outside for clearance. You were not involved with the party in the reception area. Jane did not mean anything to you except an occasional annoyance when you have tried to bypass her loops. You take offense to any suggestions that your system failed in some way. Your home life is exciting. Your wife has many inventive activities for the family to enjoy together and she keeps within a budget while planning them.

You are Lucinda. You take pride in looking for the good in everyone. When there is a failure, you want to examine all the parts to make sure it doesn't happen again. You believe that to solve problems, we first have to look at what should have been done to prevent them in the first place. You like working with computers and at times you cannot distinguish which are human components and which are developed by human components. You are not a member of the society and have often wondered if you could actually be a part of this kind of association. Not that anyone has asked. Your forward thinking is not what they are looking for, they prefer to handle damage control after the fact. You believe in rooting out the problem before it arises. You are therefore, one of the people the society avoids. You are married but have no children. Your husband is a blue collar worker and happy at his job. You enjoy each other's company and have decided to delay having a family.

You are Nelson. You talk a good line but, in fact, know very little. Your favorite saying is 'Bullshit baffles brains'. You point to the fact that you have been able to find a job in the computer field with little or no education or training. You have been able to fool the personal department, but keeping up with the facade with computer experts is another matter. Many at Star Mobile have already begun to question your credentials. Based on your resume, the society asked if you would care to join. They are beginning to doubt their decision. You are a member and you took part in the murder of Plain Jane. You were able to follow orders and do your part, but you got lucky. Plain Jane was pretty much in bad shape when you arrived. Now you will have to remain undetected with some of the experts in the field questioning you. You are an unfaithful husband which puts a strain on your family life. You put your extra marital pleasures before your family. It won't be long before you can fill all of your extra time with your harem.

You are Milton. You are not a member of the society. You know of them, but their secrecy methods border on mutiny within the company. You always believed in loyalty. The company deserves your loyalties as do your co-workers. You have left a paper trail as you pulled together your components for Jane. Every aspect of the construction of Jane has been documented. Your notes will serve you well as you sort out the problems that made the society think Jane should be destroyed. You will be a part of the team that rebuilds Jane. Your family also benefits from your loyalty. when you leave the company, you leave your work behind. Your home life is private and you do not sit around talking with other employees about it. Home and company are totally separate.

You are Lester. Star Mobile has been your life for the last twenty years. You have been involved with Plain Jane and all of her predecessors. You don't believe such drastic measures were necessary. Star Mobile keeps up with the times and that includes the updates for Jane. You are a member of the society, but you declined to be a part of this scheme, you received orders and read them. You simply told the society you would not do what they asked. Your reasoning was that it would not be long until the company replaced Jane. Patience is your by-line both at work and with your family. you would never do anything to put either relationship in jeopardy. You are secretly trying to find a way out of the society permanently. With your family you prefer the comforts of home. Yours is a close family and takes pleasure in doing things together.

You are Millicent. You gave Jane her personality and have tinkered with her output. You are very proud of your part in Jane's workings. You were aware that Jane was not perfect and that when the time came to rebuild Jane you would have to work on some of the complaints. Because the company regularly updates the computer systems, you did not consider it an emergency to work out the problems. Whoever was responsible for Jane's dismemberment caused more problems for you than were solved. Now you have to start at the beginning and hope you find the problems as you rebuild. It would have been much easier for you to correct the circuits and trace the trouble spots. You are single and lead a well ordered social life style. You like to travel and usually go places alone. Other people just seem to get in the way.

GAME #5 PLAIN JANE

Party Host: You have been invited to join in the search for the person or persons responsible for the dismemberment of Plain Jane. You should all remember Plain Jane and her cheerful offer to help you through your conversational tour of Star Mobile and the use of Jane. Last evening as many of you know Plain Jane was attacked and horribly dismembered at Star Mobile office. We will all remember her and her wonderful loops that without fail would bring you back to the beginning where you can research new areas within the Star Mobile complex circuits. Oh Plain Jane, we will miss you. How can anyone be so cruel? To leave Jane exposed to the elements and spread throughout the offices. Ladies and Gentlemen, you are the brilliant minds who conceived Jane and we appeal to you to salvage whatever we can and start anew with a larger more advanced model. How better to honor Jane's passing. We are waiting for any information that can lead us to the people who entered Star Mobile with murder in their hearts.

Party Host: Sedgewick, can we start with you?

Sedgewick: We can, but I don't know what I can tell you. I'm a computer engineer, not a programmer. I did go by the offices last night, but there were no lights on. I didn't really want to go in to work by myself. Unfortunately, Jane is not the type to have an independent conversation. "Just speak clearly into the mike and tell me what I can do for you today". The thought of having another meaningless discussion with Jane was too much for me. It was about 11 pm. And I did not see or hear anything outside or in the parking garage, I didn't go inside.

Party Host: Hollis, what about you?

Hollis: Well certainly I was in the office last night. Jane was her delightful self, kind and helpful. I didn't have time to do the 'loop de loop' with her. She didn't seem to mind my ignoring her, she just went on buzzing and talking to her callers. She did have quite a following. Several people I spoke with said that she had a way with first time visitors and made everyone feel comfortable. I didn't see anyone in the offices when I came in. I passed no one in the halls and only the usual cars were in the parking garage. I finished my work and checked out.

Party Host: Smithers, have you heard anything?

Smithers: Last night I did my best to stay away from all the tomfoolery. There was a party in reception and I was not invited. Jane did not call out for help. From what I could hear, she was rather enjoying all the attention. I saw a few people in the reception area dancing and singing. You would have thought they were having the time of their lives. At various times, they cheered some new action. I left around midnight and went down the back stairs to the parking garage. Jane was alright when I left.

Party Host: Archy, where were you? Don't you usually watch out for any problems at night.

Archy: I was just as anxious to have a good time as anyone, but they said it was a private party. I waited for the noise to calm down and I watched them leave. Jane was still answering calls so I thought all was okay. How was I to know that they could do all that to Jane and she could still talk? I didn't go into the office until this morning. Made me all but cry to see Jane like that. She spoke a few last words and just kind of faded right away. I'll never forgive myself that I didn't check on her more often last night but there were no alarms going off. Jane seemed to handle everything by herself. I liked Jane and I'll miss her.

Party Host: Zimpler, were you here last night? did you see anyone or see anything unusual?

Zimpler: I was invited to the party. While I was there, I joined in the fun. Our only aim was to see if we could trick Jane. We were all trying to ask impossible questions. You know like Spock did on the enterprise. He asked the computer to compute pi, which we all know is impossible, but the computer went nuts trying. We had some pretty good problems for Jane to figure out. She was up to the task and each time she found the answer we cheered and went on to the next. But Jane was okay when we left. We cleaned up the office, said goodnight and left. That was about 2 am. And we absolutely did not harm Jane. It must have been someone waiting in the office for us to leave.

Party Host: Elspeth, Can you shed any light on the situation? You were very close to Jane. did you enjoy the party? Was Jane enjoying party?

Elspeth: We were all enjoying the party including Jane. She was really on the ball. Figured out all the problems we gave her and seemed to relish the attention. No one at the party even spoke harshly to Jane. Things were starting to calm down when I left at 1 am. A few of us left together and went down to the parking garage. As we were driving out, I saw a different car come in, but I thought nothing of it because everyone has to have a key to get into the garage. Unauthorized cars cannot enter.

Party Host: Manley, you designed the garage entrance and exit doors, would it be possible to sneak in without a pass?

Manley: It would be very difficult, but I suppose the possibility exists. But even if they got in past the gate, they would have to avoid the cameras. Has someone checked the film from last night? If someone did come in to the garage, one of the cameras would have picked it up. Whoever our intruder was, he may have been prepared for that and blocked out the cameras. Otherwise, I don't like to point out the fact that it was someone who works in this facility. It could even be one of us in this room.

Party Host: Lucinda, you have not commented yet.

Lucinda: While I can't help thinking that Jane deserved better, she certainly did everything she was programmed to do. Maybe if we had helped her through some of the tough times, she would not have annoyed so many people. She should have had some new vocabulary and new directions for people to follow. I liked talking to Jane, but there were some days when she sent me around the same way ten times and still didn't get me what I wanted. All I'm saying is; maybe we are all to blame for what has happened. We didn't take care of all her needs so that she could expand her horizons. It's obvious that someone was very frustrated with Jane.

Party Host: Nelson, do you have anything to add?

Nelson: I know what it is like to be frustrated with Jane. One day she sent me on a merry old loop that had me half way across the country and back again to the start. And because interaction with her is close to impossible she did it again. I've heard of people who have been the circuit ten times without getting the information they need. There is no way of breaking loose and speaking to someone else. You can only hang up on her, seems rude, but sometimes that is all you can do.

Party Host: Milton?

Milton: Oh come on now. We are talking about a machine. Jane was not like anyone else. She was not a living breathing person. Let's give our heads a shake. What do you intend to do when you find who did this? Charge he, she or them with murder? The way you are talking, Jane cannot be replaced. She is after all a machine. We made her what she is today and we can do it again. But let's start all over from the beginning. We will give her a new persona and some directions that lead to the right connection faster. She won't be plain Jane anymore.

Party Host: Lester, what do you have to say?

Lester: She won't be Plain Jane anymore, but we must consider who she will be. We must also consider the fact that someone did end her life. And it's our job to make sure it doesn't happen again. Before we move forward, we have to look backwards. We can examine the parts and correct the flaws. Did Jane have too many loops? Or was it just that she was tuned into too many choices? What did annoy people who were calling in? Time is money and our clients do not want to waste time. If Jane has not found the right line within say 3 min., one of the links should dump the caller into the proper department and let the receptionist redirect the call. It's not a perfect plan, but it will work better than leaving all connections up to Jane.

Party Host: Well Millicent, you are the last, were you at the offices last night?

Millicent: I was. I had a few problem solving questions for Jane, She answered them with a sigh. Not a hint that she had any trouble answering them. We all cheered whenever she solved a problem. It was a fun time with a lot of good food and drink. We cleaned up afterwards and departed. Jane was okay when we left. I think you might even say she was quite happy. A good time was had by all and Jane was left to take care of the incoming calls in her own enchanting way.

Party Host: The time has come for some serious sleuthing. You have until I call a halt to the inquisition to find out as much as you can from the other participants. Listen to every discussion and form an opinion. Each of you has a character profile, answer questions according to how you think your persona would respond. When time is called, write down your answer: Who or what is Jane? Who conspired to end her life? What was the motive?

GAME # 6

FROM
THE
GRAVE

GAME #6
FROM THE GRAVE

THE INVITATION

Come join me as we explore the past, long, long past. My family's past and perhaps some of you can trace your ancestors back to those ugly days of witchcraft. I have found some interesting treasures from those days. I would like to share them with you Come and perhaps experience a visit from that dark other side.

DATE:
TIME:
PLACE:
PLEASE R.S.V.P

INSTRUCTIONS:

You may want to substitute your guest's names in place of the numbers. Copy the speeches and cut the speeches apart. Give each guest a speech. Be sure to have jars with ointments or colored liquids and dried weeds. Also have cookies and pop to serve.

Party Host: Attics can be dark, mysterious adventures and I had waited a long time before I could explore ours alone. I really was not interested until my mother received some old trunks left to her from her mother. They held deep, dark secrets from our family's past and now I wanted to find out what was hidden there. My mother added to the mystery by forbidding me to ever open those trunks. But today she was out visiting and the rest of the family had other things to do.

I stood at the foot of the stairs for what seemed forever. That cold, dreary staircase finally beckoned me to venture into the attic to look for that ancient trunk and drag out the secrets my mother was so afraid to reveal. As I ascended the stairs, I felt my stomach lurch. Not just the normal dust and cobwebs made it seem dark and dismal, but there was the added stench of old, very old materials. As I made my way pass the junk too precious to throw out, I could make out the trunks hidden away in a dark corner. The large room seemed to close in on me, warning me not to go further. A few times, I was sure I could see someone watching me, but I was determined. I must know the family long hidden secrets and that thought alone pushed me onward.

The trunks were unlocked but were sealed with heavy leather straps. I carefully worked the buckles loose on each one. There was nothing that would evoke such fear as my mother showed, when talking about them. I closed the trunks just as I found them and finally came to the one that was from my ancestor, the witch. Great … great grandmother Lydia was, according to the stories, a fearful old hag, who cast spells and cursed her enemies. She even cursed her own family should they discard her possessions. She vowed to revisit the family and forever cause sorrow for who ever would disturb her belongings. She would not allow them to rest as long as all that was hers were not as she had left them.

I paused only a few moments as I loosened the straps. I could hear a low moan and began to feel a cold draft about me. Should I go on? I came this far and I was not going to get another opportunity. The old hinges creaked as I opened the lid. Inside were the old woman's possessions. I couldn't find anything frightening or unusual until I pulled open the drawer at the back of the trunk. There were dried up weeds, small bottles that had held ointments and liquids and, at last, a book.

I picked up the book and again heard the low moans and some shrieks, but nothing could stop me now. I opened the book and gently turned the pages. There were recipes for old spells, curses, and lists of those people who would do her harm. Old hags who were thought to be witches were treated badly in her time and she yearned for revenge. She wrote about the people and how she would make them suffer for the pain they had caused her. Her own family shunned her, feared her. She boarded herself up in an old cabin and avoided the rest of the world and now in opening her trunk after so many years, I was setting her free.

Time, I hoped, would soften her cold heart. I had an overwhelming sense of sorrow for this woman, who for so long needed compassion. Would she understand how I felt? I closed the trunk and took her book with me. I wanted more time to examine it, more time to learn about Lydia. And so, dear friends, I thought we could have an evening of mystery and adventure. I have brought in many of the ingredients of some of her old ointments and I planned to make a few. In her book, she has recipes and directions for using them to the best advantage. Whether she wanted to harm someone permanently and scar them for life or if she only wanted to cause them a little discomfort.

Belladonna could be added to food and cause cramps and stomach upset. It could also cause death. Mix it with lard and it became an ointment. The effects when applied to the skin were quite relaxing. It was how a witch went to Sabbath. It was not a physical trip, but an hallucination. They would fall into a deep sleep and upon awakening felt refreshed, saying it was the best sleep ever. The only recipe I tried is the ointment so if you want to try it, use a little bit, don't overdue it.

I have some really neat plants to sniff. They are mainly very pleasant aromas that can help you sleep or relax. Plants like sage, lavender, rosemary, wild garlic, cedar and juniper. And any of these can be boiled in a tea.

1. Hmmm, I could get used to some of these. Where did you find them? I love the lavender. If you can get the plants, I would like to make a small garden of them.

2. I don't know, the old witch was pretty upset. She may have written some things in those recipes to lure people into drinking them without knowing it was poison. This book could be her way to get revenge.

3. Oh come on! Do you think she would plan to murder her own family and anyone else who would read her book? She was just putting the fear into them.

4. Okay, so tomorrow we take the book to a pharmacist to have the ingredients checked out. Tonight we just sniff the plants and maybe put the ointment on our hands.

5. No, no, no! I won't have anything to do with it. That old lady deserves our respect. She may not have had the power to cast spells or curse people, but she was trying to tell her family how

much they hurt her. They forced her to live like a hermit and shunned her. I think cursed or not, we should leave her belongings in that old trunk.

6. Oh, wow! Did anyone else hear that wail? I've never heard the wind make those sounds before. Maybe we should put everything back. I don't want an old witch mad at me. I don't take chances with the things I don't understand.

7. Let's at least try a little sniff. It's not like we are sniffing glue, these plants really have pleasant aromas. I'll try the ointment, I am not going to eat it, just rub it into my hands.

Party Host: My mother baked some cookies today. She knew that some friends were coming over to have a party. She baked quite a few so enjoy. I have some pop in the refrigerator. While you are munching, you might want to look over the weeds and the ointment.

8. Oh good, I love the cookies your mother bakes. Mine makes them from a roll or a bag. but never from scratch. After this sugar fix, I just might try some of that ointment.

9. Did Lydia write about anything besides her rotten family? Can you imagine her own family being so mean? I read that old women were labeled witches without any proof. These old women were herbalists who helped to cure some illnesses with their knowledge of plants. It's too bad they were misunderstood in their efforts.

Party Host: I guess she didn't have a chance. Whenever she left her small cabin, her neighbors threw rotten vegetables and stones at her. Her family was not much better. All she had were cold empty rooms, not even a pet to keep her company.

10. I was looking at the list of names in her book. Many of them seem familiar, is that a coincidence or did she live in this area?

Party Host: I tried to find some of the people in the library. A few may have ancestors who lived here at one time, but it was hard to find a paper trail to connect them to each other. I wonder if any of these families had strange unexplained problems. Did Lydia get her revenge?

11. I don't know, but right now I feel a little dizzy and I have an upset stomach. Does anyone else feel sick?

Party Host: I have stomach cramps. Did you hear that? It sounded like laughter, strange and kind of eerie.

News Update Of the 12 young people who apparently took ill at a party, only 2 remain in hospital. Police have indicated that it was food poisoning and are looking for the source. None were seriously injured and the party host was also poisoned. There may be an outside source responsible.

Party Host: It is decision time. Who did it? What was the weapon? What was the motive? Did Lydia somehow come back from the grave to help or was the murderer deranged? Write down your answers and place your ballot in the bowl. The winner will be chosen from the correct ballots.

SOLUTIONS

GAME#1
THE BIRTHDAY PARTY

Daughter Tilly was the murderer. She had for fifty years taken care of her parents. She had no life of her own and yearned for one. The weapon was scented candles on the birthday cake. Yorek died of anaphylactic shock when he blew out the candles. Tilly did not succeed with her total plan. She had hoped that the shock of Yorek dying would give Mattie a fatal heart attack.

GAME #2
THE STORY BOOK CAPER

Although there were a lot of people angry with the murderer, Red Riding Hood. They also thought she was a thoughtful child. She was a selfish child who would do anything to get what she wanted. Her main aim was to murder her grandmother, but she would settle for any one of the ladies. Why did she want to get rid of grandma? Grandma kept her date, the woodsman, busy and she missed the prom. Grandma wanted fresh flowers often and Grandma wanted her company often. Red decided to use a hat pin dipped in poison to do the job.

GAME #3
THE PERILS OF FAITH

Calvin, poor Calvin, just never knew when to quit. Trying to murder Faith so he could collect her fortunes, was motive enough, but then he tried to gain public support by accusing her of causing the accidents. It was too much for Jasper to take. Jasper had been a faithful employee of Faith and her father for many years. Get rid of Calvin and you get rid of the problem. While Jasper was wandering around the room talking to the many people there, he planted his poison. The poison was in the candies he so generously handed out. Oh, don't worry he was careful to keep Calvin's favorite candies separate. Those he put on a dish in front of Calvin on the stage. By the way, has anyone seen Jasper lately?

GAME #4
BARNWICK HUMBUG

Good old Barnwick. His family for years has supported him, but this time his idiot proposals have become too much. Harlow sat around listening to the family as they discussed what to do about Barnwick. In his feeble little brain, he thought of a great final solution. He would shoot Barnwick and blame it on the sheriff. Bad plan. The sheriff might have been mad enough, but he was nobody's fool. It was Barnwick who kept him employed. Harlow borrowed a gun from the sheriff and waited for him to leave the studio. He then shot Barnwick while he was on stage. He was sure that the sheriff would return to pick up Barnwick, but he didn't plan on Mike to do so many errands while he was gone. Mike was a mama's boy and he left to buy groceries for mama, feed mama's cat and talk to mama for a while. Now what mama's boy do you know, would be able to leave mama after a short talk. It would take several minutes and he would not have had time to shoot Barnwick. Harlow's plan to take over from Barnwick became a dream while he pondered his mistakes in prison.

GAME #5
PLAIN JANE

Plain Jane was a telephone answering machine. As soon as she answered the telephone, she would ask callers to make a choice of four options, then she would follow it up with another set of options, and then another. She was oblivious to the number of options and choices and to the number of times she sent callers off on the same quest only to return to her again and again. The secret society, of course, planned the demise of Plain Jane, but who carried out the deed. The conspirators were Sedgewick, Zimpler, Elspeth, and Nelson. These people were more than annoyed with the workings of Plain Jane. That's why when approached by the society, they agreed to eliminate the faulty computer system. Screw drivers and wrenches do a wonderful job on unsuspecting computers.

GAME #6
FROM THE GRAVE

The mother of the party host baked special cookies with haunting ingredients for the occasion. She wanted to punish her daughter for having invaded Great … Great Grand mother Lydia's privacy. When the young people gathered together to share in her daughter's findings, mother was furious. She decided that they all must be punished. She delighted in the moans and shrieks that seem to come with the wind, Lydia was here. She was sure that Lydia returned from the afterworld to help her. Her lawyer is entering an insanity plea.

978-0-595-43705-4
0-595-43705-2